D1261822

THE SINGING LEAF

Pedro wants very much to play music with the trio at fiesta time but he doesn't yet know how to play the guitar. One day, when Pedro is collecting wood in the forest, he meets an old man who is making beautiful music on a laurel leaf. The old man teaches Pedro how to play the leaf and soon Pedro learns the lovely *Jarabe* dance.

At the end of this easy-to-read story you will see if Pedro was good enough to play with the trio.

E.
Row

A SEE AND READ

Beginning to Read Storybook

THE SINGING LEAF

by Florence Wightman Rowland

Illustrated by Earl Thollander

G. P. Putnam's Sons   New York

IMMACULATA COLLEGE

HAMBURG, NEW YORK

24,522

To my sister, Virginia

Second Impression

Text © 1965 by Florence Wightman Rowland
Illustrations © 1965 by Earl Thollander
Library of Congress Catalog Card Number: 65-20713
All rights reserved
Printed in the United States of America
Published simultaneously in the Dominion of Canada by
Longmans Canada Limited, Toronto
06208

Whent Pedro saw the dark woods not far
away, he went faster. Soon he would be out of
the sun. At times it got very hot under the sun
of Mexico, but the woods were cool. The woods
of Mexico had many tall trees and pretty flowers
and singing birds. The people of Mexico loved
to sing, too.

5

Pedro was tall for a boy of ten. But it would be a long time before he was as tall as his father. Like his fat, jolly mother, he had a round face and a happy smile. In his black eyes there was always a look of fun.

Before long Pedro was walking into the woods that shut out the hot sun. Nearby a bird sang from the top of a tall tree. How pretty! How *very* pretty!

After the singing stopped, Pedro began to whistle. He sounded just like that bird.

Every day Pedro came here to get wood for the family fire. As he walked along, he thought about the Fiesta. Today there would be a Fiesta in the town of Gata.

People would be coming from far and near to play games and to dance. Pedro did not like to dance, but he liked to hear the music. Best of all he liked the *Jarabe* dance because it had happy music.

Today Pedro walked on and on and on. Before he could go home, he had to find enough wood for his family. If this took too long, he would not have time to get to the Fiesta.

Pedro wanted to hear the trio, those three men who played music together. When the music was happy, Pedro's foot would go tap, tap, tap in time to the melody.

At the last Fiesta, the tall man, the biggest man in the trio, had smiled. "Do you play?" he asked Pedro, and he started to hand the boy his guitar.

Pedro shook his head from side to side. "I — I do not know how to play a guitar — yet! But someday I hope to make music as fine as yours."

"When you know how," the man said, "come to Gata. You may play with our trio so that all can hear your guitar music. Would you like that?"

Delighted, Pedro said, "I would like that very much."

Time after time Pedro thought about these men and about what the tall man had said. Would he get to play with that trio someday? Would he? But how? There was no money in the family to buy a guitar.

Today it took Pedro a long time to find enough wood. At last he had enough to make up a big bundle. By then the sun was about ready to set. He knew the Fiesta would be over long before he could walk to Gata.

15

Unhappy, Pedro started home with the bundle of wood on his back. As he went along, a bird sang from a treetop. But he saw no bird. Then he thought: That is not a bird after all. A bird did not make *that* sound. *That* sound is new to me.

Hoping to find out what it was, Pedro turned off the road. Not far away he saw some laurel trees. That new sound was coming from behind those trees.

When Pedro came nearer, he saw a small hut. It was not as big as the hut he lived in. Out front were two chairs. An old man sat in one of them under a laurel tree.

The pretty sound stopped as Pedro came up to the hut. The old man called out, "Hello there. Sit down, boy! You look hot."

"I am, Señor," Pedro said, putting down his bundle of wood. "Did you make that music?"

"Yes, I was playing on a leaf."

"A leaf?"

"Yes! I pick a laurel leaf when I want to play some music." Then the old man went on to say, "You can do it too," and smiled.

"I, Señor?" Pedro asked. "But let me see you do it first. Can you play the *Jarabe?*"

"That's easy," said the old man, and he played the fast, jolly tune.

When the music stopped, the old man picked a leaf for Pedro. "Now you try it," he said. "Hold the leaf between your thumbs, so! Push your thumbs against each other — hard — so the leaf will not fall out. Now put the edge of the leaf to your lips and cup your hands as I did."

Pedro did everything the old man said. He put the leaf between his thumbs and pushed them together. Then he put the edge of the leaf against his lips.

"Cup your hands more," the old man said again. "Put the fingers of one hand over those of the other."

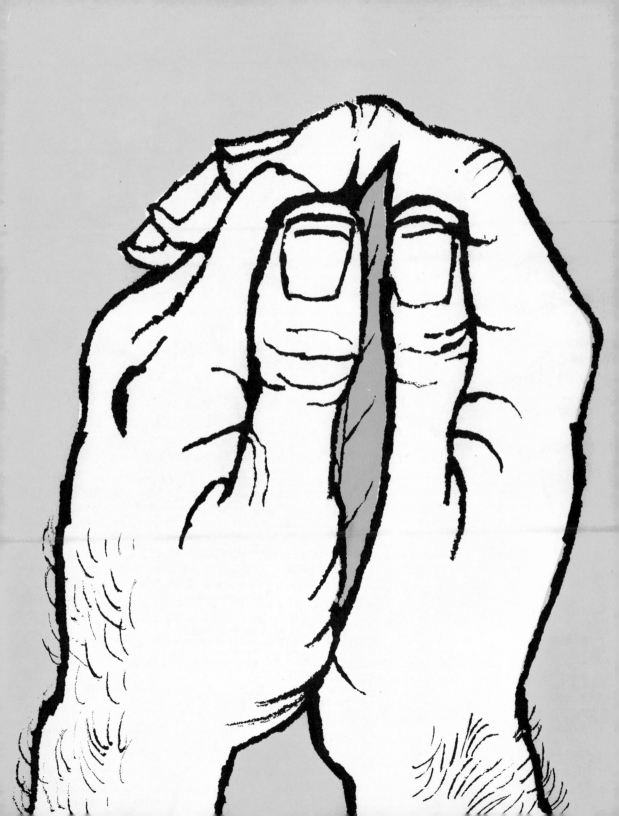

F
Row
24,522

Pedro moved his fingers and rounded them, the leaf still up to his lips.

"There, now you have it," the old man said.

Pedro blew and blew and blew! But the sounds he made were not at all pretty. "It is hard to do," he said without smiling.

IMMACULATA COLLEGE
HAMBURG, NEW YORK

"You will soon know just how to move your thumbs and fingers. It is very much like trying to whistle. Someone can tell you *what* to do, but not *how* to do it."

Over and over again Pedro blew on the leaf. Still the sounds were not right.

"I think you try too hard. Take it easy, boy!"

When Pedro tried again, the old man said, "Now that is more like it."

This was fun. Pedro did not stop until the sun had gone down behind the high hills. He jumped up. "I must go," he said. "We have a laurel tree at home. I'll try to make music on a leaf every day. Thank you for showing me how." He picked up his bundle of wood.

"Good-bye, Señor."

The next morning Pedro did his work in the fields. Then he went to get wood for the fire. When he came back home, he sat under the laurel tree. His two little brothers were playing nearby.

As Pedro blew on the leaf, the boys ran up to him. One asked, "What are you doing?"

The other said, "It sounds like a hungry goat to me," and they both began to laugh.

Pedro had to laugh too. "You are right," he said. "It is not good yet, but it will be someday. I must try harder."

Just then their mother came to the door, holding the baby by the hand. "What did I hear? Are you boys hurting one of my chickens?"

Pedro's little brothers laughed so hard they fell to the ground, rolling over and over.

"I was playing music on a laurel leaf," Pedro told his mother. "Soon it will sound pretty like the old man's music." Then he told her what happened the night before, on his way home.

The happy days flew by for Pedro as he made music on a leaf. After many, many days had gone by, he knew his music sounded pretty. Best of all, his brothers did not laugh at him anymore.

Once when he was playing the *Jarabe,* Mother came out of the hut. She put one of Father's big hats on the ground. "Start that over again. I want to dance." And she did!

When the music was over, she said, "You do just fine, Pedro."

Now Pedro knew he was ready to see the old man. Hoping to surprise him, he stopped by the next day. "I came to play for you," he said.

It did not take long for Pedro to play the *Jarabe*. Then the old man said, "Your music pleases me."

Then Pedro told him about the three men. "Am I ready to play with that trio, Señor?"

"You are ready, and I'll go to Gata to hear you. There will be another Fiesta three days from now."

Those three days did not go by fast enough for Pedro. But at last the happy day came. The sun was up and so was Pedro, long before any of the others. He called out, "Up, everyone. Get up. This is the day I'll play with that trio in Gata. But there is much to do before we can go."

"Why do you get up so early?" Father asked. He sounded cross.

Mother said, "If you were ten, you would be in a hurry, too. You would want to get an early start."

After breakfast, Father said, "I'll not work in the fields today. I'll go with you to get the wood for our fire, Pedro. Then we will walk to Gata."

Pedro was glad to have Father's help. They came back long before twelve. Then they ate the food Mother had ready for them.

After that, Mother said, "Put on a clean shirt, Pedro. I want you to look your best at the Fiesta."

Pedro pulled off his old shirt and took one off the door hook. It was the white shirt he put on to go to church on Sundays.

In the yard, Pedro picked five laurel leaves and put them in his pocket. Now he was ready

to go and so was the family. They started up the road together.

In Gata they made their way to the street where the trio always played. And there they were. Many people had come to hear them.

After the music stopped, Pedro walked up to the tall man. "At the last Fiesta, Señor, you told me I could play with you."

"That I did," he said. "Here is my guitar."

"But — but —" Pedro began, "I do not play a guitar, Señor. I play a leaf. A *laurel* leaf."

"A leaf?" the tall man asked, just as Pedro had once asked the old man.

"Yes, Señor!" Pedro took a leaf from his pocket. "I can play the *Jarabe* on this laurel leaf."

"That I have got to hear," the tall man said. "Go on! Play your leaf. When you are ready, we will start."

Pedro smiled. At last he was going to play with the trio. He had worked so hard on his music; if only he would play well now!

Pedro turned to face the people. When he looked at them, his hands shook. As he put the leaf between his thumbs, it fell to the ground. A few children laughed.

But Pedro did not let this stop him. With hands that still shook, he took another leaf from his pocket. This time he did not drop it. He put the leaf between his thumbs and up to his lips. Then he began to play the *Jarabe.*

As Pedro blew on the leaf, more people stopped by to hear him. Up front, near his family and school friends, stood the old man. He had come to hear Pedro play, just as he said he would.

Pedro did his best. The *Jarabe* filled the street with its lively music. How lovely it sounded with the trio playing along!

No one turned to go away. They all looked at Pedro, standing where they were as he played on and on. How he wished the *Jarabe* were a longer dance! How he wished it could last all day!

When Pedro saw many people tap their feet to his music, that pleased him. He knew they must like it very much. Nearby a little girl was doing the *Jarabe* dance with her brother's hat. Her little feet moved fast in time to the music.

After the *Jarabe* was over, everyone clapped and clapped and clapped their hands. Pedro had never been so happy before. He smiled at them, glad that they liked the music he made on the *singing leaf!*

Key Words

blow (blew)	finger(s)	lips
between	foot	music
clap(ped)	guitar	shirt
dance	hut	tap
edge	laurel	thumb(s)
eye(s)	leaf	trio
		tune

Spanish Words

Fiesta (fee-ES-tah)

Gata (GAH-tah)

Jarabe (hah-RAH-bay)

Señor (sen-YOR)

The Author

FLORENCE WIGHTMAN ROWLAND taught a writing course at Pasadena City College in California but gave it up when it interfered too much with her own writing. With *The Singing Leaf,* the author's published books, all juveniles, number six.

A former resident of California, Mrs. Rowland is presently touring the United States, together with her husband, in a twenty-six-foot trailer.

The Artist

EARL THOLLANDER began serious training as an artist at the City College of San Francisco and subsequently attended various colleges for art training. He is an avid traveler and especially enjoys working "on location." The artist has a number of juvenile books to his credit, the last one for Putnam being *Jump Frog Jump.*

Mr. Thollander, his wife, and their two children live in a house which overlooks San Francisco Bay.

AG 2

DATE DUE